AF527427

BFF TRAP

The New Friends

Ruby Geller

RED INTENTIONS PUBLISHING

A modern romance story

First Published in **June 2025**

ISBN: 978-93-6356-284-4

RED INTENTIONS PUBLISHING

+91 9311101365

Distributed by: Watergies

Preface

In a relationship, the key to make it work is to know how to react in which situation. Yes, sometimes you need to take a stand for what you believe is right, but when the situation calls for it, you should be willing to apologise even if you are not wrong. There might be compromises you might have to make, but it is only you who will bear the rewards.

Foreword

The author takes you through a chance of fate where forgiveness is on the cards, but an ultimatum comes along with it. When the result is almost a clean slate, would you do whatever it takes. A short, entertaining story that makes you ask yourself whether you would do what he did if you somehow screw up.

Acknowledgments

A heartfelt thanks to the publishing team for everything you have done for William, Fiona and Jerome.

About the author

Do not screw up with me. Even if I love you, I might still make you pay.

Dedication

This one is dedicated to William, for being the bigger guy in the relationship and working to make it work even if he does not think he is at fault. It took courage to do what he did, but perhaps forgiveness was worth it.

Introduction

Imagine yourself working up to an apology even though you believe you are not at fault. Sometimes a simple sorry can solve a lot of problems if ego does not find its way, or in this case fate does not play another prank. How far do you think you would go in order to deescalate an unfortunate problem with the love of your life. Will you really do anything they ask or would you finally say enough is enough. Continuation of a modern romantic story between two best friends, William and Fiona, where William's one victimless mistake changes everything about their lives. It all happened because he crossed a line and she laid a trap. Find out what happens with their new friend after she laid the BFF Trap.

Prologue

"We can keep deliberating on this, waste enough time on trying to move on or we can actually move on right now. I mean we both want to do that eventually, so why waste precious time on what we both know we want. Sharon is gone, there is nothing holding us back anymore. Whatever misery came into this relationship with her, it should leave with her as well."

"William, it is not that simple. I don't think you are realising the gravity of the situation here."

"I am, but I believe in us more."

Contents

Chapter One
Chance

Lying down alone on the bed, William knows he is in deep trouble. For the first time, he knows he has screwed up. All the other times when fate played a prank on him, he knew he was at the wrong place at the wrong time, or it was something involuntary, getting carried away with the situation, but this time, he knows he is wrong. He had a chance to come clean, but he thought he would get away with it. He knows he has crossed a line, and he is going to have to face the consequences.

Fiona was furious, and he knows anytime now, she is going to call him downstairs, and he is going to be ashamed to even look her in the eye.

After thinking about the situation for another half an hour, he hears what he was dreading, Fiona calls him form downstairs, “William, come here.”

Nervously, not even caring about his nakedness, he walks downstairs, and with his head hanging lower again, he goes and stands in front of the television, facing Fiona sitting on the couch.

She says, "William, you are not going to utter a word, you are just going to shut up and listen. I have tried everything with you. I have tried being mean, I have tried being soft, I have tried locking you up, I have tried giving myself to you. I am out of options, I am out of patience. I don't have the strength anymore to work on your life. It is clear you cannot be trusted. Not only can you not be my partner, right now, you cannot even be my friend. I have had it upto here. I am just not willing to make an effort anymore. I first thought that I should actually beat the shit out of you for what you did, but what is the point ? I might put you through any number of miserable situations, I might strip every bit of self respect you have, but in the end, you are just going to do something to let me down yet again. You are going to do whatever you can do to break my trust. I have never in my life hated anyone more than you do. That is not because I don't hate people, it is because I genuinely cared for you, and you let me down every chance you ever got. I sometimes feel that you go out of your way to hurt me. Look at the things you have done, how many times have you broken my heart. I let you stay alone at home, you broke into my underwear drawer, sniffed my panties, wrapped them around your cock and jerked off. I let you clean my wardrobe, trying to teach you a lesson, you mess around with my vibrator. I try to supervise your touching yourself, giving you your privacy, and you make me stand in your cum. Whatever I do, you make it miserable for me to even bear the sight of you. I mean, how dare you sleep with Sharon while I was in the other room. I am sure you are going to blame it on her, but where do you get the balls to do that ? She could not force herself on you, you had to be a willing participant. On top of that, you have the courage to lie to my face after I ask you point blank. You know I wanted to give you every opportunity, every benefit of doubt, I asked you repeatedly that did you have anything to tell me, and you did not utter a word. Then, I asked you whether you slept with Sharon and you blatantly refused to my face. Have you got no loyalty, no respect for me ? I mean I thought you were just a guy who was high on hormones, and once all is said and done, you can turn out to be a gentleman, but I cannot believe how wrong I was. Everything you had done till now, that was between you and me, but this, this is cheating, and I draw the line there. I know I cannot not only date you anymore, but I cannot even live with you as housemates, let alone friends. William, you and me, we are done, we are over. I never in my life want to see your face again. You broke my heart, and there is no one else who has ever done that. I decided on not even letting you speak a word, but for once, you did actually shut up and listened. So, I am going to give you one opportunity to explain yourself. This might very well be the last conversation we would ever have, so do me a favour and don't lie to my face. Just be honest, so at least I can leave with one honest memory from here. Speak up now. Start."

Chapter Two
Explanation

William was not sure where he should start, but he knew it was now or never. He realised this was about to be the most important conversation of his life, and while he is always smitten around Fiona, owing to his love for her, in this moment, he did not care what she thinks about him. He only cared about an honest conversation, being true to her and himself. He did not care if that turns out to a conversation of love, of care, of hatred or of resentment, all he cares about was expressing his emotions, getting his point across.

He says, "Fiona, I am going to start by saying I apologise. Whatever I am about to say, it does not excuse my actions, but it does provide a justification. While a justification does not make it excusable, it does provide a true evaluation of circumstances, reflecting I had no choice in the choices that make you resent me right now. I know whatever relationship we have been in, it has been tiring as well as trying for you. To say the least, I might have definitely exhausted your patience. I believe that you have the truest of intentions, and coming up with the things that you have come up with, it definitely takes a lot of planning, and presenting it as in the moment, it makes it even harder. I genuinely thank you for whatever you have done for me. While all these experiences might not have been as pleasant as I like, but each of them were definitely a memorable one, something that I am not going to forget until the day I die. I am sorry if I have let you down on multiple occasions. Let me assure you that it was never my intention. I love you more than life itself, and I have loved you since forever. I am not ashamed to admit that, I am rather proud of making my choices known. This relationship might not survive, but I can be proud of the extraordinarily amazing choice I made. You are my best friend, you have been with me through thick and thin, and when any sane woman would run away after catching me for the first time, you stayed. You were definitely pissed, but you stayed, in order to make me a better man, and I chose to believe I am indeed a better man because of you. You are the world to me, but if you want to leave, I am going to respect that, and let you go without uttering another word, because I will respect your choice. But before you take that decision, you need to know things from my point of view as well. You brought Sharon in on whatever this is, without even asking me. You let her take control, you gambled with her keeping me as the stakes, you made out with her in front of me, you made out with me in front of her, you let her make out with me in front of you. I am not just ashamed of the things we have gotten into, I am disgusted. I never expected you to go this far. I was willing to understand you wanted to try new things, and subconsciously, I had a sinking feeling that this would be one of those things, but involving someone we both know, that too so intimately, it crosses all lines. I wanted to protest, but you never even gave me the chance. You made me open the door naked after just screwing me. Moreover, you told her not to sleep with me. You did not even think of tell me not to sleep with her, how am I to blame for something that you never even told me about. You just lost me in a bet, and told me to do whatever she asks of me. How am I ever to understand where you drew the line in your mind. I am sorry, but I am not sorry for that. What I am sorry for, is lying to you after the fact. But, Sharon put me in an impossible situation. After sleeping with me, she told me that you specifically asked her not to sleep with me, and then she told me that if I did not want to break your heart, I cannot tell you about it. What is a guy supposed to do in that situation. What had happened, had happened, and I wanted to protect the situation once Sharon had gone.

Yes, I did not want you to know that I slept with her. I genuinely thought that this was the best course of action, and if you want to penalise me for it, so be it. But, don't even think of telling me that you cannot trust me or all that shit. If anyone is responsible for all this, it is you. Not Sharon, not me, just you. You had no right to gamble me, and you know that, and if you willingly did it anyway, it is for you to face the consequences, and not me. If you want to leave, there is the door, walk out, but you are not going to walk out of there thinking that I was at fault, and you did not screw up this time. I know I am being straight, but it is high time someone told you that actions have consequences. I screwed up, and I faced mine. The question is, are you willing to face yours ? The rest is upto you. I have nothing further to say, but just apologise once again for any intentional or unintentional way I might have hurt you, because that was never my intention."

Chapter Three
Text

Fiona stares at William blankly for a minute, still not believing that he talked to her this way. After all this time, she did not think he had it in him. He thought she had broken him beyond repair, but standing naked in front of her with a half boner, she cannot be more attracted to him right now. She also knows that if she gives in to her needs after this, it is going to change the dynamics altogether, and if she even walks out of here, it will be useless, and all she would be doing is giving up the perfect home for no reason. She is actually speechless when it comes to arguing his reasoning. She knows she needs some time for a good comeback if she is ever going to get a hold of the reins of this relationship.

Fiona says, “William, that was a lot. I need time to think about things. Clearly, I was just looking at my side of things. I need to reevaluate everything, but I cannot do that if I am looking at you. I am going out. I am going to text something very specific, and I need you to be doing that. Can you handle that one simple thing ?”

William replies, "Of course I can. I have been doing that all the time. It is you who needs to be clear about what you want me to do, since you are not willing to live with the repercussions."

"You have already made your point, you do not need to gloat about it."

"Alright."

Fiona picks up her handbag and she walks out. Standing naked in the middle of the living room, William feels empowered. He took a stand for the first time, and he left her speechless. Lying down on the couch, he screams with joy. When he was lying upstairs on the bed, he never thought that this situation could possibly have this result, and he is proud of how he handled it.

After lying down in front of the television for an hour, he rushes to the kitchen, and taking out the panties Sharon left him, he goes upstairs to hide them on top of the wardrobe. After all he has said, he does not want this coming out and screwing things up again.

He is startled by a text from Fiona – 'I am still pissed, I am still hurt. But, I have come to see things from your point of view. I am not saying that I am forgetting it, I am not saying that I am forgiving for it, I am not even saying that I am not going to bring it up again. But, I am willing to go back to things as they were before Sharon came. If you are as well, you will go in my room i.e. your old room, and inside the wardrobe, behind the hanging dresses you are going to cuff yourself, both hands on separate rods, and both feet on separate bars. Along with that, you are going to gag yourself so that you cannot speak even if you want to. You are going to leave the wardrobe open, but you must not be seen from behind the dresses. If you are willing to do this, I am too. All the cuffs are in the dresser, bottom drawer. If you don't, then it is actually goodbye. You have ten minutes.'

Reading the text, and getting a deadline of ten minutes, William knew that he had no time to think of possibly what she could have going through her mind. He rushes upstairs, and first gagging himself with a ball gag, he cuffs his feet on opposite ends, and then after cuffing his left hand, but realises that he cannot cuff his right hand, so he bends and uses his cheek to cuff his other hand. Once locked, he wonders what if she actually left. He would die cuffed in here, hiding behind the dresses and no one would find his body for months. The thought scared him, but he knew she would come back for him if she hears nothing. She might not show, but she loved him too.

Chapter Four
Watch

Waiting for a few minutes, he hears the entrance door open. In anticipation of something kinky coming his way, like it usually does, he gets hard. Whatever she might do with him, he knows that he is going to enjoy it in this predicament.

As she come upstairs, he is shocked to see her holding a man's hand. He thinks to himself that getting another person involved is the reason they are in this situation, and she went ahead to involve another one.

Without even looking for him, but seeing the wardrobe open, she knows that he is inside. She starts kissing the man, and they take each other's clothes off. He was unable to move, not sure what that would accomplish. She might have obviously told the man that he was cuffed there in the wardrobe, and that is just going to add to the humiliation.

She gets down on her knees, and starts blowing him. He was disgusted to watch him sucking another man's cock, but what choice did he have now. He silently just stares at her.

After going at it for about five minutes, she gets up on the bed, and getting down on her hands and knees, she gets in position for him. The man spanks her ass, and then inserts his cock in her. As she lets out a gasp, she winks at William. She could not see him, but she knew he was staring at her. The man starts thrusting in her, and she swirls her tongue on her lips, showing William how much she was loving it.

William was stunned, but he could not help feel his cock grow. It was like watching an adult video, but with your girlfriend as the star. The man goes harder and faster at her, and she moans at the top of her voice while constantly staring at the wardrobe. Although he was well hidden, he could still feel her staring into his soul.

After a few minutes, she pushes the man on the bed, and kissing him for a minute, she gets up on top of him, and she starts riding him. She ensured that he lied down facing the other side so she could continue staring at him.

William wanted desperately to stroke himself, and standing behind her dresses, he knew he was ruining one of them with the constant flow of precum. He was disgusted and excited at the same time. Disgusted, because that was the woman he loves, doing another man right in front of him, and excited because it was of course the woman he loves doing something erotic.

Pushing her up, he pulls her down and stands to insert his cock in her once again. Fiona did not plan on this position, but she pushed her head backwards to ensure that

William was looking at her face, and she moaned as loud as she could.

A minute later, her moans got erratic and louder, and he knew she was cumming. Screaming at the top of her voice, she let go. The man increased his pace of pounding her after hearing her moans, and within seconds, he came too.

After a few more thrusts, he fell down over her, and rested his head on her breasts while his cock was still in her. While the man was lying on her with his eyes closed, she continued to smile at William.

William did not know how he is going to react once the man leaves. He did not even know what this was. Was it still over, and this was her way of saying goodbye, or was this some sort of revenge sex, or was it a part of her new experiences, or was this just some kind of a punishment. He decides to let her take the lead in the conversation and reply according to what this actually is.

Regaining his composure, the man gets up and kisses Fiona.

She says, “You were good.”

The man says, “You were amazing, but I thought you were dating someone. I was going to ask you out before, but they told me you were in a relationship.”

“Well, it is complicated. Would you like a drink ?”

“Just one. I have to get back to work soon.”

Chapter Five
Revenge

William stares at the man lying naked on his old bed, and Fiona comes in with two glasses of wine.

The man says, "Well, tell me how complicated it is."

Fiona says, “I can introduce you to him, and you can figure out for yourself.”

“Just to brighten up my chances, I look forward to it.”

“Aren’t we confident enough ?”

“Just willing to take a chance.”

“Yeah right.”

“No, I actually like you.”

“I am not sure that this is going to go anywhere. Like I said, I am in a complicated relationship.”

“I don’t see the guy around, I am willing to take a leap.”

“Well, I am sure he knows what I have been upto.”

“I doubt that, no one lets a woman as beautiful as you go around screwing guys.”

“You will be surprised as to how persuasive I can be.”

“I would like to be surprised.”

Fiona kisses him and says, “This is enough surprise for one day.”

“Happy with it. Tell me about yourself, other than persuasive, what are you ?”

Looking at the wardrobe, clearly conveying the message to William, she says, “I am someone who does not like to be messed with. I don’t want anyone messing with my belongings, I don’t want anyone disrespecting me. I will let a lot go, but if you screw me over, oh honey, you are so screwed.”

The man says, “Intriguing, go on.”

“I am just your next door neighbour. Kinky, sweet, hot, that about sums it up.”

“Kinky, sweet and hot. What else does a guy need.”

“You would be surprised as to how far guys would go to screw things up.”

“You were right, it does seem complicated. I got to head back now. Call me ?”

“Sure. Count on it.”

Kissing her again, the man dresses up and they both head downstairs.

William hears the door close again, and he knows that at least one of them has left. He hopes they did not leave together.

Hearing Fiona come up the stairs, he knows his moment of reckoning is here.

Fiona comes in the room, and pulling the dresses to the side, she says, "You really are a pervert, aren't you ?"

Taking out his ball gag, she asks, "Did you really get hard looking at me being done by him ?"

William asks, "Fiona, who the hell was that guy and what are even you upto ?"

"Firstly, you screwed someone else, I did that too. I was in the other room, you were in the wardrobe. I saw you doing Sharon, you saw me doing Jerome. I think we are even, and by how turned on you are, I should have let you join us I suppose."

"Fiona, this is not the same thing. You lost a bet to Sharon, I did no such thing. Moreover, getting another person involved is what got us in this mess in the first place, and you did that again anyway."

"No love, digging into my panty drawer got us in this mess. I am just trying to get us out of it."

"Fiona, you are crossing another line."

"Just like you do all the time ?"

"You know this is different."

"Yes, this is different, you know why I did Jerome in front of you, because of the way you talked to me. You had no right to scream at me. If I never took that from anyone, let alone you before, I am not going to start now."

"I was not screaming, I was just telling you the facts."

"Well, I too am not sorry for sleeping with another person."

"Fiona, open me up."

"No, you are going to stay here for a few hours."

"Fiona ?"

"Good night love, I will see you tomorrow."

"Fiona, I am sorry."

"What ?"

"I am sorry."

"Why ?"

"For screaming at you."

"And ?"

"For saying this was your fault ?"

"And ?"

"For sleeping with Sharon."

"And ?"

"I don't know what else. I have said everything I could possibly think of."

"Are you sorry for disrespecting me ?"

"I never disrespected you."

"Well, I felt disrespected. Maybe you realise it after a few hours."

"No, no. I am sorry for disrespecting you."

"Thank you, was that so hard ?"

William just looks down with defeat, and Fiona opens up his cuffs. Stepping out while feeling strange pain in his body, William says, "My body hurts. I think I am going to take a nap."

"Yeah, I am sure Sharon wore you out."

"Fiona, can you let it go ?"

"Not anytime soon. I still need to process it. But, I don't still want to see your face right now. Go, take a nap or something. I will see you tomorrow."

"Gladly."

Chapter Six Morning

William wakes up still thinking about Jerome and Fiona, no matter how much he tries to get that image out of his mind, he just cannot. He feels that Fiona crossed a line and there is no coming back from it. He still loves her, but he is not sure whether he can be with her anymore. To his surprise, as he opens his eyes, he sees Fiona lying next to him.

Last thing she told him was that she did not want to see his face, and now she came in sometime during the night to sleep in his bed. He does not know how to react, so he just lies down and stares at her sleeping calmly like everything is perfect in the world.

Within a few minutes, Fiona wakes up, and opening her eyes, she just smiles at him and says, “Good morning Wendy.”

Not wanting to start the day with a fight, he says, “Good morning Fiona.”

Fiona says, “I was missing you, and I did not want to talk to you, so I sneaked in here, I hope you don’t mind.”

"No, of course not."

"So, we should talk about what happened yesterday."

"I don't know what you want me to say. You crossed a line."

"Oh, so as long as Sharon was involved, that was fine, but if I got Jerome, that crosses a line ?"

"Fiona, I knew Sharon, you knew her. This was an unknown guy you involved."

"Jerome is not an unknown guy, I have met him a few times. If things did not turn out how they did with us, I would have been probably dating him."

"Yeah, you did screw him anyway."

"Do you want to talk like adults or are you going to be a teenage girl ?"

"Are you even listening to yourself ? Do you realise the depth of what you did ?"

"Wendy, did I sneak into your wardrobe to sniff your panties and wrap it to jerk off ?"

"Fiona, we are done with that. You cannot bring that up every second."

"I can bring it up as long as I feel violated."

"And having me handcuffed, hiding in the wardrobe while you screw another guy does not violate anything ?"

"It is less violating than screwing our best friend while I was in the other room."

"Fiona, you involved her, I did not."

"Listen William, I am not going to apologise for what I did, but if it gives you any comfort, my feelings for you have not changed. I can still keep up with what we have doing, you can still work up to earn my forgiveness, but it does not change anything."

"I don't think so .."

Fiona interrupts him and says, "But, don't you ever dare talk to me the way you did again. I let it go once, I might not be that understanding again."

"I had to explain myself, someone needed to show you the mirror."

"And how did that work out ?"

"You are impossible."

"William, do you still love me ?"

"I guess so."

"You guess or you know ?"

"I know."

"Alright then, I have the same feelings for you, but even if you ignore the whole Sharon incident, consider it a part of me trying something new with a person where there are no strings attached."

"And what was the point of making me watch it ?"

"That performance was directed to you. I did him for you."

"What are you even saying ?"

"I am saying that I wanted you to see me with another guy. Obviously it turned you on. You did spoil my clothes leaking precum in the wardrobe."

"It was like watching an adult video."

"And you have been always a pro at it. So why do you mind ?"

"Are you even listening to yourself ? I was not watching a random girl with a random guy. I was watching the girl of my dreams, my girl screwing another guy. I don't think you are mature enough to realise what you did. You are just a spoilt girl who has taken my love for her for granted, and you crossed a line from where it is not going to be easy to come back."

"William, you know I came in here to comfort you. I thought that I should help you through it, but I forgot what a hypocrite you are. You screwed Sharon, and while you have your explanation of things, the fact remains that you did screw her without me in the room, and then lied to me about it. At least I did not do anything behind your back and then lie to you about it. I guess coming in here was a bad idea."

"You put me in the room with Sharon."

"And you could have stopped her. She did not force herself onto you. You know what, I am out of here. I am going to my room. Come see me when you get some realisation about who is more wrong here. I just cannot believe you."

"Fiona .."

Fiona just gets up and walks out the door ignoring his calling out her name.

Chapter Seven
Realisation

Lying in the bed, watching her leave, William knows that he just lost this conversation. He thought he had the upper hand, but as she walked out, he lost whatever advantage he had. He still thinks that she did wrong, but to deescalate the situation, he is going to try and apologise to her. He knows he will have to keep self control if things are ever to calm down, and for Fiona, he can throw away his ego and do anything she wants.

Getting up, still naked, but wearing just a chastity cage, he knocks on the door to his old room.

Fiona says, “Come in.”

As he enters in, she asks, “What do you want ?”

William replies, “Just wanted to talk.”

“Well, I don’t feel like talking to you.”

“Fiona, I am sorry.”

“You are sorry for what ?”

“About Sharon of it.”

"I am listening. Last time we talked about it, you said it was all my fault."

"I think it is neither your fault, nor mine."

"If that is the case, then why are you apologising ?"

"I just want us to get back to normal."

"And how do you think that is going to happen when you believe I crossed a line while I gave you the taste of your own medicine ?"

"Fiona, can we just be rational about it and try to put this behind us ? We both are pissed about something or the other, but it about both of us and nobody else. Whatever happens, it will happen to us. If we enjoy being with each other, it will be for us. If we are miserable with each other, it will still be with us. Can we try and understand each other and move on from this ?"

"I thought you were here to apologise. I am listening."

"Alright, I am sorry for lying to you about it. Rest of it is still is a grey area, but I should never have lied. We need to trust each other. I got carried away with Sharon's thought process, and I should not have. I really love you Fiona, and I don't think lying is the way to show that to you."

"See, was that so hard ?"

"Harder than you would know, since I have my reasons to defend it."

"Shut up, don't go there. We will be back to square one. So, you have no resentment ?"

"I do. I hated what happened with that guy. Please don't do that ever again."

"Okay, I will keep that in mind. No promises though."

"Why ?"

"Because unlike you, I don't lie to you."

"I already apologised for it, didn't I ?"

"Wendy, you have apologised for a lot since I have been here, but this one hurts the most. I know the other things you did were far more creepier, but you were being just a guy I suppose. You crossed a few lines, but I believed that was your infatuation with me, but this one, this was not at all about me, but rather about betraying me. I don't know whether I have it in me to forgive you for it, let alone trust you ever again."

"I am wiling to work for it, I am here apologising for things that I do not even fully agree are my fault, that is all because I love you and I want to be with you. I don't care what it takes, I want to move on from this. I have no ego about it."

"So you are going to keep your feelings about this bottled up ?"

"No, I am going to forget about it in order to move on. What we have is far more important that what happened."

"What if Sharon shows up again ?"

"I will leave it upto you to decide the best course of action."

"So you trust me ?"

"Fiona, more than I can ever trust myself."

"Strong words, I must say."

"Stronger feelings."

"William, I am just not sure about it. You have betrayed my trust every time I have turned around."

"I know, but look at me, what I am wearing, this is me trying to regain your trust. I am willing to do whatever you say, what can be a better leap of commitment than that ?"

"I suppose you are trying, but even when you were trying to make up for your screw ups, you did not hesitate to screw up again, just because you thought you would get away with it."

"What I did, I did not know that was wrong, honestly. I really thought you allowed her to have her way. When I lied, I was just doing damage control. It was never my intention to hurt you."

"Any yet you did that anyway."

"And here I am, owning up to it, apologising for it."

"William, I really want to be pissed at you. I want to punish you, make you pay, but hearing all this, I don't think I can."

"So you can forgive me instead ?"

"I wouldn't say we are there yet."

"How do we get there ?"

"Go downstairs, make some breakfast. I need to think about a few things, call me when it is ready."

"Sure, what would you have ?"

"Just some cereal and milk."

"Okay."

"I will be down in ten minutes."

"Alright."

Chapter Eight
Ultimatum

Walking downstairs, William knows he did alright. This situation could have led to very different results, but he found her soft corner, and he made his way in. Now, whatever she decides, it might be difficult momentarily, but it will be over soon. This entire episode will be in the past, and they can go back to where they were.

He heats up the milk, and keeps the cereal box on the table. He knows he is almost out of the water, and if nothing wrong happens during breakfast, the situation would be neutralised.

Fiona comes downstairs and takes a seat at the table.

William brings up her milk and asks, "Would you like a toast or a sandwich ?"

"No, I think I am fine."

"You think or you know ?"

"Very funny. Come, take a seat."

"Sure."

William joins her on the table and says, "So, did you think about it ?"

"I did."

"And you forgive me ?"

"No, I don't yet think that you have felt what I felt."

"Fiona, watching you with another guy was realisation enough."

"Like you said, it was like watching an adult video. If you have no idea what I am feeling, how would you even relate to it ?"

"I don't know, but I think if we move on from it, we will be fine."

"Yes, in the short run. But, you will have bottled up feelings, and unfortunately, so will I."

"So talk to me. Tell me what you feel, I think that will help."

“I just cannot describe it in words. I am sorry, I don’t know what to do.”

“Fiona, I am here to listen. I am willing to work with you on it. Can I be candid ?”

“Sure, of course.”

“We can keep deliberating on this, waste enough time on trying to move on or we can actually move on right now. I mean we both want to do that eventually, so why waste precious time on what we both know we want. Sharon is gone, there is nothing holding us back anymore. Whatever misery came into this relationship with her, it should leave with her as well.”

“William, it is not that simple. I don’t think you are realising the gravity of the situation here.”

“I am, but I believe in us more.”

"It is just not that simple."

"We can make it simple. I am here for that."

"Alright, there is one thing in my mind that can assure me that you feel the same way that I did."

"Of course, anything. Just name it."

"Don't be so sure about it."

"Fiona, like I said, I am willing to do anything."

"Since you played with me and Sharon, I suppose if I get to play with you and Jerome together, I believe I will be able to move on."

Dropping his spoon on the table along with his jaw, William asks, "What ?"

"I am serious."

“Are you kidding me ?”

“I will be able to forgive you then, and moreover, I will be able to cross something off my list.”

“Fiona, that is just not possible. I am yours, and I am not at all comfortable sharing you with another guy even if I am in the room.”

“Something along the lines of how I felt when you were with Sharon.”

“You were calling the shots then, you were gambling with her.”

“Whatever, that is what will make it okay.”

“I don’t know what to say.”

“If you want me to forgive you for what you did, this is how it will happen.”

"Are you giving me an ultimatum ?"

"If you want to call it that, sure, I am giving you an ultimatum."

"What if I refuse ?"

"We get miserable. I never forgive you, and eventually we will drift away."

"Do you want that ?"

"Do you ?"

"No."

"Then what is one uncomfortable night for my happiness and forgiveness. Put your love to the test."

"That is not how love is proven."

"It is how it is with me. Anyone can come up with an apology. To know whether you actually mean it, you need to get out of your comfort zone."

"Are you sure that is the only way ?"

"After thinking it over, I think there is no other way. To never get into this kind of a situation again, I think you need to experience it."

"Fiona .."

She interrupts him and asks, "Did you not say you would do anything ?"

"You know I did not mean this, I meant anything for you."

"And this is for me. The choice is yours. All of this can be in our past today itself. The question are you willing to go the extra mile to prove your love ?"

"This is not the extra mile, this is something else altogether. I don't think I have it in me to do a guy."

Fiona bursts out laughing and says, "Oh, you are not doing him. You will do only what I say, and I promise it will not be him."

Thinking for a minute, William asks, "And he won't do me ?"

"Nope."

"Alright then, if that is what it takes to earn your forgiveness, let me prove my love to you."

Fiona jumps in her place, and moving in to kiss him, she kisses him passionately and says, "Thank you for this, you really are the best. I already texted Jerome, he should be here in a few minutes."

"When did you text him ?"

"Before coming downstairs."

"What ?"

"Wendy, I know you better than you know yourself."

Chapter Nine
Apology

Speechless, William wonders whether he is that predictable. It was almost impossible for him to take this decision, but Fiona knew what he would decide before she even asked the question.

Fiona says, "I think I should remove that chastity cage. I don't want him to tell anyone that you I keep you locked in. I mean, I don't mind that, but then I would have to tell the reason why, and I am sure you don't want that."

William replies, "Whatever the reason, I am happy if it comes off."

"Alright then, stand up."

As William stands, Fiona takes out the key from her anklet, and opens the lock to the cage. She removes the penis cover and then pulls on the ring to remove it from his balls.

Watching his cock grow with her touch, she says, "Looks like you are excited about Jerome."

"No, I am just relieved to come out of the cage."

Fiona's phone rings and she says, "He is right on time."

"What ? He is already here ?"

"Yes, and unless you want to go open the door, go into my room and wait for us on the bed."

"Fiona, there is still time. Think about it."

Chuckling, she says, "I did, and I like it."

With his head hanging low, William goes upstairs and sits on the bed. He is unsure as to what position he should sit in. He finally decides on sitting facing the window so that he is not on display as soon as they enter.

A minute later, he hears them come up and instantly regrets accepting it all.

The door opens and Jerome asks, “Woah, sorry man.”

Fiona laughs and says, “Wait, he is here waiting for us.”

Jerome asks, “What ?”

“Yes, and he won’t cause trouble.”

“I don’t think I am comfortable with that.”

“Then there is the door, you can walk out. But, if you want me, that is how it is going to be.”

“Sure, why do I care ? I am sorry man.”

Fiona kisses him and removes his t-shirt. Jerome returns the favours and they both remove each others clothes while still kissing.

Fiona gets down on her knees and starts blowing him. Continuing to suck him, she snaps her fingers and gestures William to come to her.

Knowing he has already crossed over, William stands up and walks to them. She holds his hand and continues sucking Jerome.

Fiona takes Jerome out of her mouth and says, “Get on your knees with me.”

William complies and sits with her. She sucks him a few more times and holding William’s head, she pulls him closer and says, “Taste it.”

William protests, “No way.”

Fiona says, “I was not asking” and she pushes his head in.

William reluctantly opens his lips and takes Jerome’s cock in his mouth and sucks on it once.

Fiona asks, “How is it ?”

With a disgusted face, William just coughs.

Laughing, Fiona says, “You have got to ready him for me, keep sucking.”

She pushes his head in again, and with no more strength to refuse anything, he sucks on Jerome’s cock as she guides his head.

After a few minutes, Fiona pulls him back and says, “Leave something for me too.”

Holding both their hands, Fiona takes them to the bed and she climbs over Jerome to take him in. She starts riding him while still holding William’s hand.

With a smirk on her face, she asks, “How do I look ?”

William does not know how to respond to that question, and just stares at her blankly.

After another minute, she playfully slaps William and says, "Stroke yourself, slowly. Don't cum."

William starts taking his hand up and down his shaft at a very slow pace, and Fiona starts riding Jerome faster.

Jerome lifts her up, puts her on the bed and getting on top of her, he starts going deeper and faster.

William tried to comfort his mind that he was watching an adult video, but he knew his body was betraying him. He hated every second of this, but he could not help get turned on.

Fiona winks at him, and bites her lip before starting to moan. She moans for a minute, and then bending forward to come inches away from his cock, she keeps her hands on the floor while still keeping her legs on the bed.

Watching her take the position excites Jerome more than he imagined it would. He immediately starts pounding her, and going as fast and hard as he could, he showed no restraint. Fiona started moaning again, and she was moaning right over William's cock. William did not know how long he would last, but Fiona starts screaming at the top of her voice, and grabbing William's cock, she digs her nails in and cums. Hearing her cum, Jerome went even faster, and within seconds, he cums into her.

William was feeling everything he could every feel. He was disgusted, turned on, humiliated, in pain, and on the edge. He knew if she would have just grabbed him instead of digging her nails, he would have cum by now, and he would have been in a much more difficult situation, trying to prove how disgusted he was inspite of everything else.

Chapter Ten
Forgiveness

Panting, Jerome falls back on the bed and William is just glad that his nightmare is over once and for all.

Fiona says, “Jerome, time to go.”

Jerome asks, “What ?”

"I have him to take care of."

"Rude, but I understand. Sorry man."

William is still confused as to what is happening. He knows no matter how much he is turned on, he cannot do sloppy seconds. Silently, he waits for Jerome to dress up and Fiona kisses him as he leaves.

William asks, "Is it over ?"

Fiona smiles and replies, "Almost there. Get on the bed."

"Fiona, I cannot do him after he has filled you up."

"Oh, then you better clean me."

He did not understand what she meant, but without warning, she climbs up on the bed and sits on his face.

William jumps his legs in protest after realising what she wants him to do. But before he could get out, Fiona grabs his cock and he and instantaneously loses his will to protest. He calms down and Fiona says, “Lick.”

Coming this far, he just wants to get over with everything. He realises there is no point in backing out now, and he digs in. He can taste Fiona’s delicious juices, but he gags on Jerome’s cum. Fighting through it, he keeps on licking.

To his surprise, Fiona starts stroking him, and she was going fast. She was not teasing, but she was actually going to make him cum. Suddenly, Fiona leaves his cock and pulls it to his stomach.

He did not realise what she was doing, but he was enjoying it. She playfully slaps him in the same direction twice, and he was getting closer. He did not want this to be one of the best orgasms he has ever had after all he has been through, but he was feeling ecstatic.

Fiona starts stroking him again, and then she pulls his cock towards his stomach again. She shakes his balls, and then pulls on it again. She starts stroking for three seconds, and pulling it again repeatedly. He could feel his cum shaking in his cock, and then as he was on the edge, she pulls it and just leaves it altogether.

No matter how much he tried to control himself, he could not stop the cum from coming out. It just bounced all over his stomach, and Fiona while laughing pulls his cock again.

She gets up while still laughing and rolls on the bed alongside him. She says, “Now we are done.”

“Did you have to ruin it ? I was having the time of my life, and now I cannot help feel the urge again.”

“Awww, look at your face. It is red with embarrassment, and is glowing with cum.”

“Fiona ..”

“I really thought that the first thing you would say would be a comment on Jerome, but now I am sure that you always think with your little brain. Anyway, all is forgiven,”

“I suppose all’s well that ends well.”

“Let me correct that, the Sharon part is forgiven. You still have to answer for all those things that came before that.”

“Fiona, can’t we just start dating like normal people ?”

“Wendy, we are never going to be like normal people, not after all we have been through, but that does not mean we cannot be together.”

“But ..”

“No buts, just be glad that this part of our life is in the past, that this is the best outcome of all this, just take the win.”

“Sure, but it does not feel like a win.”

“Let it sink in. Once you start thinking with the brain in your head, you will be able to taste it.”

“Taste ?”

“Oh, I am sorry, you tasted something else altogether. How did it taste though ?”

“I do not even want to answer that right now.”

“Fine, you will answer it later then. Now, go take a shower. Then lock yourself up, and prepare me a good meal. I am famished, I need lots of carbs.”

“Okay.”

Grabbing his hand, Fiona says, “I think I might fall for you Wendy.”

William says, “Sure” and with shame on his face, he walks out of the room.

Epilogue

William feels disgusted and humiliated, but what she did with her hands, he just cannot get over it. He felt pleasure hitting him in ways he never thought were possible, and if she had not let go of him at the last moment, that probably would have made to at least the top three, if not the top. He knows that woman is magic to him and there is not a lot he would not do for her. What he did today, he never even imagined that in his worst nightmare, but before even asking the question, she knew that he would not protest. He knows all of it is not over, but at least the Sharon part of it is. Little does he know that another secret is about to come out, and although most of it would have already been forgiven, keeping a secret might not be that easy. Will William let Fiona continue to push him in ways he never thought were possible, or will he again try and take a stand. After yesterday, he knows that sometimes taking a stand will help him get his away, but there might always be repercussions to it. Will Fiona finally fall for him or a secret is about to land him in even more troubled waters ? Read what happens next in William and Fiona's life in 'BFF Trap - The New Respect'.

www.ingramcontent.com/pod-product-compliance
Lightning Source LLC
Chambersburg PA
CBHW062111160726
48282CB00026B/758